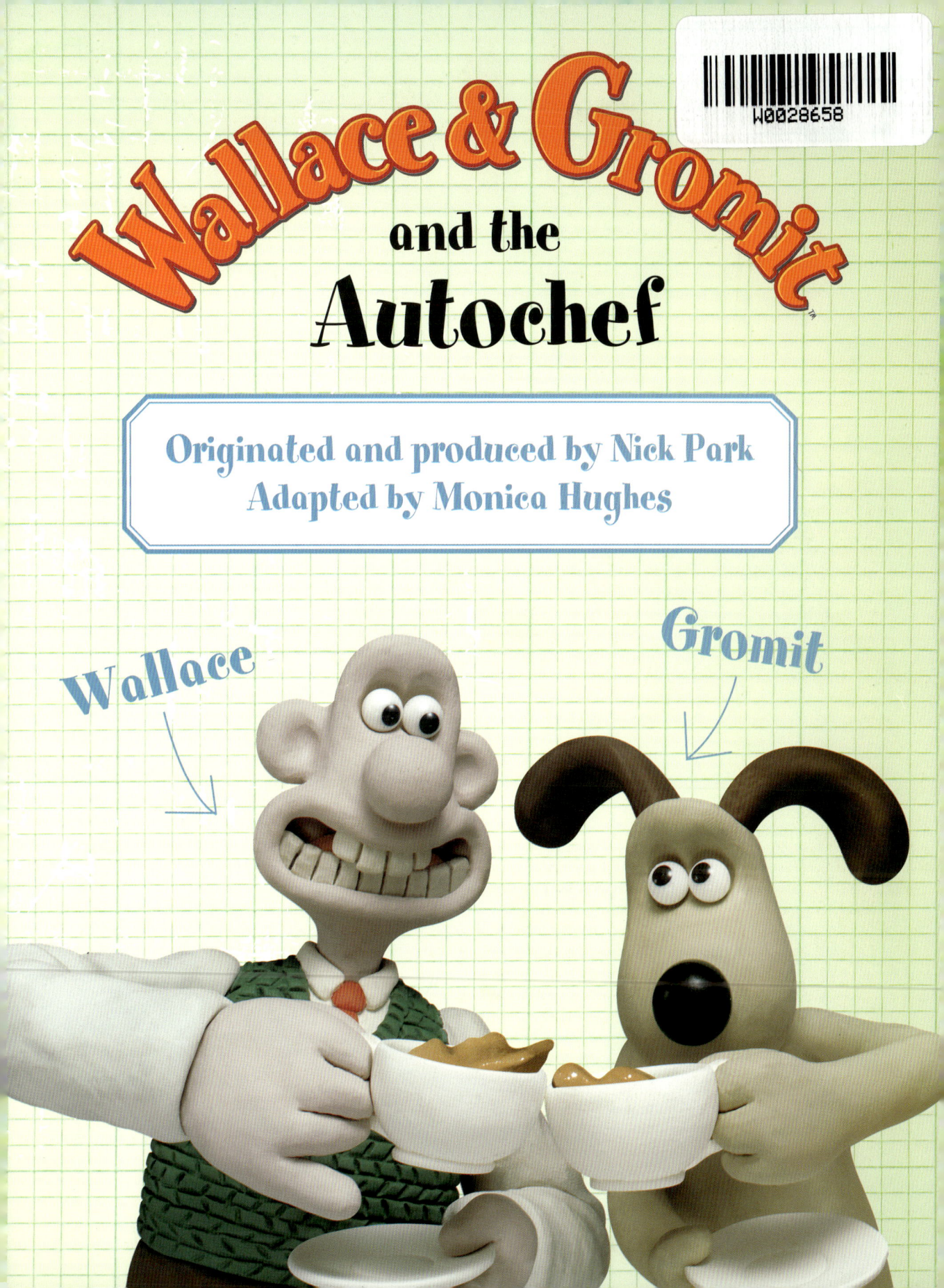

Wallace was trying to fix the remote for his new invention, the Autochef!

I think it will work now, Gromit.

Gromit put on his raincoat and his hat, just in case the Autochef did not work!

There was a loud beep and the Autochef came out of the kitchen. It was a robot!

Beep!

Beep!

The Autochef could make breakfast.

How do you like your eggs, lad?

Wallace pressed a button on his remote.

The Autochef began to cook the eggs.

The top of the Autochef popped up and the eggs shot out …

Wallace pressed a button on the remote again.

The Autochef began to fry the eggs.

They looked very good.

Just then, the eggs shot out of the Autochef.

This time they hit Wallace in the face!

Ah! Ah! Help me, Gromit!

Next, the Autochef began to make the tea. But the tea shot out of its spout!

The Autochef spun round and round. Tea went all over the place!

Do something, Gromit!

So Gromit stuck a banana skin on the end of the spout.

Then the Autochef went mad!

It spun **round** and **round.**

The top shot off and steam came out.